MR HENRY
and the
SEA
SERPENT

Scholastic Children's Books,
Scholastic Publications Ltd,
7-9 Pratt Street, London NW1 0AE, UK

Scholastic Inc.,
730 Broadway, New York, NY 10003, USA

Scholastic Canada Ltd,
123 Newkirk Road, Richmond Hill,
Ontario, Canada L4C 3G5

Ashton Scholastic Pty Ltd,
PO Box 579, Gosford, New South Wales,
Australia

Ashton Scholastic Ltd,
Private Bag 1, Penrose, Auckland,
New Zealand

First published in hardback by Scholastic Publications Limited 1992
This edition published, 1993

Text and Illustrations copyright © Andy Ellis 1992

Andy Ellis has asserted his moral right to be identified as the author of the
work in accordance with the Copyright, Design and Patents Act 1988.

ISBN 0 590 55273 2

Printed in Hong Kong by Paramount Printing Group Ltd.

MR HENRY
and the
SEA
SERPENT

Andy Ellis

Hippo

For Mark and for Cornwall

Mr Henry lived in a cove by the side of the wild ocean. When he was young, he had spent his days fishing far out on the salty sea. Now that he was old, he preferred just to lie in his boat and read as he bobbed about in the water. Sometimes he would fall asleep and dream of days long ago.

One day, while he dreamed, a mischievous wind slipped the rope that held his boat to the quayside and carried him past the tumbling tide and far out onto the wild ocean.

"Wha . . .what's going on?" he cried, as a splash of water woke him up.

When he looked out, dark clouds were hurrying by above him. Huge waves rocked his little boat and the wind howled.

Mr Henry was startled by a face peering over the side of the boat. It was a seal and it looked very frightened.

"Come in, my dear," said Mr Henry and with a bit of a struggle, he hauled the seal into his boat. He wrapped it up warmly in his big sea coat.

Then a puffin blew, flapping
and squawking, down to the
boat. Mr Henry lifted the corner
of his coat and the puffin hopped
in next to the seal.

The storm grew wilder and lightning flashed all around them. "Who's this?" thought Mr Henry, as two black flippers appeared. He reached out and pulled a little penguin into his boat. It waddled over to join the puffin and the seal.

Mr Henry was beginning to wonder what was going on when something brown and furry leapt out of the water and landed SPLAT on his head. It was an otter!

It wriggled all over him, licking his face and barking loudly.

"Stop! Stop!" called Mr Henry.

"Ouch!" cried the otter and turned round to see a big, pink crab clutching onto his tail. It snapped and cracked its claws and then it scuttled off.

Despite the storm, Mr Henry chuckled to himself.

"Next thing you know, there'll be a sea serpent wanting to come aboard!"

Above the sound of the storm there came a loud SPLASH! and the front of the little boat was pulled down into the cold waves.

"Help!" cried everyone together and they all tried to hide under Mr Henry's coat.

As they watched, a great, furry head rose out of the water.

"Er . . . I was just wondering if there was room for one more in your little boat?" said a very bedraggled polar bear. They all helped him aboard, even though it was a bit of a squash.

Suddenly, the seas around them started to boil and bubble. From deep down in the darkest depths and deeper than the blackest fathoms came a sea serpent! It burst from the water, hissing and snorting and staring at them with cold emerald eyes.

"Who dares disturb me from my slumbers?" he roared.

Everyone in the little boat was silent.

Even the stormy sea grew still.

"We didn't mean to wake you," whispered the otter.

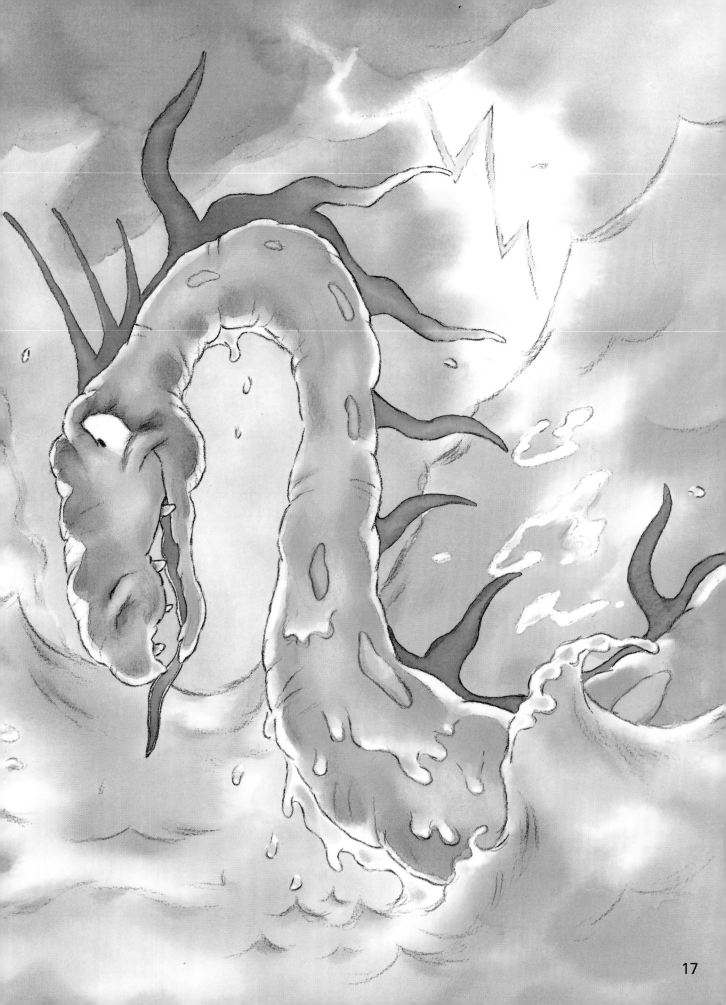

The serpent came closer and licked his lips with a slippery blue tongue.

"He's going to eat us all!" squeaked the penguin.

"Perhaps he's already had his lunch," sniffed the polar bear, who was trying hard not to cry.

The serpent smiled an awful smile and opened his huge jaws. Everyone in the little boat shook with fear as his jaws opened wider and wider and wider, then suddenly . . .

Mr Henry couldn't believe his ears!

"Th..th..that sounds like a nasty cold you've got there," he stammered.

"Yes!" sniffed the serpent, surprised that anyone should care, "and my beautiful blue spots have turned to a horrible pink colour, too."

"If I remember rightly," said Mr Henry bravely, "there's an old cure for sea serpents with sneezes and sore throats. Trouble is," he said, scratching his head, "I can't rightly remember what it is."

"First, find a pearl from the ocean deep," snapped the crab.

"Second, some shells where the old ships sleep," sang the seal.

"Third, some sand where the blue whales sing," barked the otter.

"And fourth, a feather from a seagull's wing," squawked the puffin.

"That's it!" cried Mr Henry.
"Well done, my dears," but they didn't hear him.
They had already gone to look for the ingredients.
All except the polar bear, who was too worried about being a sea serpent's lunch to think about cures for colds.

A little while later the seal flopped back on board the boat with a splash, its mouth full of shells. The puffin flew down with a feather in its beak. The otter swam alongside with some sand clasped tightly in its paws.

Mr Henry put the ingredients in his flask of hot lemon tea. The crab scuttled over and dropped the purest pearl into the

mixture. Then Mr Henry screwed the top on tightly. Now to pour the mixture into the serpent's mouth.

He thought for a moment. Then he had a wonderful idea.

Mr Henry
balanced
on the polar bear's
shoulders, the seal
balanced
on Mr Henry,
the penguin
balanced
on the seal's nose
and right at the top,
the crab
sat on the otter's head!

"Ready?" cried Mr Henry and he gave the flask a shake. A bright yellow vapour came out as he took off the top and passed it all the way up to the crab.

The crab held it carefully in its claws and poured the mixture into the serpent's mouth.

"Gloop, gloop, gloop," it went, down the serpent's throat. Everyone held their breath.

"Ahhh," sighed the serpent, "that feels so much better!" He watched as his horrible pink spots turned back to a beautiful blue again.

The polar bear gave Mr Henry a big hug.

Then, one by one, he and the otter, the seal, the penguin and the crab jumped back into the water and disappeared. They were no longer afraid of storms or gales, or even of wild sea serpents!

Mr Henry looked up at the serpent.

"Do you think you could help me find my way back to my little cottage?"

The serpent gave him a fearsome smile.

"Hold tight!" he roared.

He grabbed the bow rope in his mouth and dived into the sea. He twisted and twirled, pulling the little boat behind him. They bounced through the spray, skipping from wave to wave. Soon Mr Henry could see his cottage again. The serpent brought him past the tumbling tide and into the cove, by the side of the wild ocean.

The serpent stayed for supper, but didn't eat more than his share.

The moon was sparkling on the waves as he slipped deep down to the bottom of the sea, to go to sleep again.

28

And at night, when Mr Henry is tucked up in bed, he listens to the roar of the ocean through the window. And sometimes he wonders if the roar he hears is the sound of the wild sea serpent roaring in his dreams!